JP

Lewison Lewison, Wendy
Cheyette

Shy Vi

Shy Vi

Shy Vi

BY WENDY CHEYETTE LEWISON
ILLUSTRATED BY STEPHEN JOHN SMITH

SIMON & SCHUSTER BOOKS FOR YOUNG READERS
Published by Simon & Schuster
New York   London   Toronto   Sydney   Tokyo   Singapore

SIMON & SCHUSTER BOOKS FOR YOUNG READERS
Simon & Schuster Building, Rockefeller Center
1230 Avenue of the Americas, New York, New York 10020
Text copyright © 1993 by Wendy Cheyette Lewison
Illustrations copyright © 1993 by Stephen John Smith
Original concept developed by Parachute Press, Inc.
SIMON & SCHUSTER BOOKS FOR YOUNG READERS
is a trademark of Simon & Schuster.
Manufactured in the United States of America

10 9 8 7 6 5 4 3 2 1

Library of Congress Cataloging-in-Publication Data
Lewison, Wendy Cheyette.
Shy Vi / by Wendy Cheyette Lewison; illustrated by
Stephen John Smith. Summary: Violet the mouse speaks so softly
that her parents try self-confidence lessons, voice lessons,
and acting lessons to help her overcome her shyness.
[1. Bashfulness—Fiction.   2. Mice—Fiction.]
I. Smith, Stephen John, ill.   II. Title.
PZ7.L5884Sh   1992   [E]—dc20   91-39658   CIP
ISBN 0-671-76968-5

To Teddy and Brooklyn
—WCL

To my mother and father,
with love
—SJS

*V*iolet was a shy little mouse who had a large family.

She was so shy that she wouldn't tell
Brother Bob he was standing on her tail.

She was so shy that she wouldn't tell
Sister Sue to stop snoring in her ear.

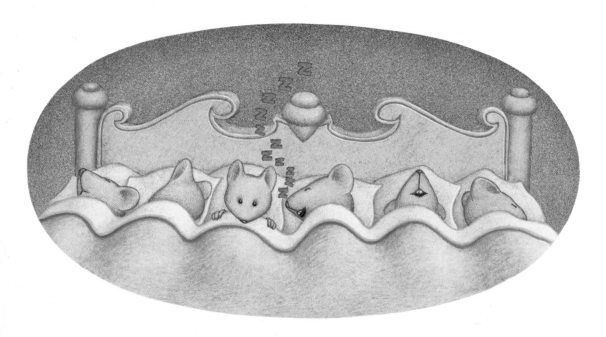

And even when Violet did have something
to say, she would speak very softly, like this:

"Please may I have another piece of cake?"

"Can I play?"

said Violet very softly.
"Speak up, Violet," said Mama Mouse.

"I'm getting wet,"
said Violet very softly.
"Speak up, Violet," said Papa Mouse.
But the more Mama and Papa Mouse told
Violet to speak up, the softer Violet spoke
and the shyer Violet felt.

"We must do something to help our Violet,"
said Mama Mouse one day. "She's too shy.
She has no self-confidence."

"Then she must have self-confidence
lessons!" announced Papa Mouse.

Violet did not want self-confidence lessons,
but she was much too shy to say no.

So the very next day, they took Violet to a
famous teacher of self-confidence.

He showed her how to
hold her head up high.

He showed her how to
shake hands.

He showed her how to master difficult tasks.

But when the self-confidence lessons were
over, Violet went up to the teacher and said
very softly, like this:

"Good-bye."

"Violet still won't speak up," said Mama Mouse. "She has such a tiny voice."

"Maybe she needs voice lessons," said Brother Bob.

Violet did not want voice lessons, but she was much too shy to say no.

So they took her to a famous teacher
of voice.

"Now repeat after me," the teacher said to
her. "LA LA LA LA LA."

And Violet said very softly, like this:

"La la la la la."

"In my opinion," said the famous teacher
of voice, "your Violet has a very fine voice.
She does not need voice lessons."

Violet nodded her head and smiled a
big smile.

"What she needs is acting lessons," he said. "Acting lessons—and a play. Yes, a play to be in. Then she will speak up."

So they enrolled Violet in Madame Beatrice's acting school, where she could learn to act and be in a play.

And Violet was much too shy to say no.

Every day, Violet went for her acting
lessons.

Madame Beatrice showed her how to bow
and curtsy. She showed her how to smile and
say thank-you.

And every day, the play got nearer and
nearer.

Everyone at home thought Violet would be very nervous, but a change had come over her.

"See how Violet poses in the mirror!" said Mama Mouse.

"She doesn't seem even one bit worried," said Papa Mouse.

"The acting lessons must be working," said everyone together.

Finally, the day of the play came.

The Mouse family arrived at the theater. Violet would have to speak up very loudly indeed in order to be heard in this big place.

Suddenly, the lights dimmed. The voices hushed. The curtain went up, up, up.

On the stage was Violet. And when the Mouse family saw her, they knew why she had not been worried about having to speak up in a play.

Violet was a flower—a violet, of course. And, of course, as a flower, she did not have to speak even one little, tiny word.

"Violet is just as shy as ever," said Mama
Mouse and Papa Mouse.

But they gave her a standing ovation. And
Violet was so pleased that just for a minute
she forgot she was shy and spoke up very
loudly, like this:

"THANK YOU!"

And very softly, like this:

"Very much."